Robbie R

# Make Mine with Everything

## Heather Sander

To Nathan
Happy reading
Heather Sander

ORCA BOOK PUBLISHERS

**National Library of Canada Cataloguing in Publication Data**

Sander, Heather, 1947-
Make mine with everything / Heather Sander.

(Robbie Packford ; v. 2)
ISBN 1-55143-308-7

I. Title.  II. Series: Sander, Heather, 1947-  .  Robbie Packford ; v. 2.

PS8587.A327M34 2004          jC813'.6          C2004-902149-4

**Library of Congress Control Number:** 2004105088

**Summary:** Robbie embarks on his second alien adventure, this time
to save the president of Kerbosky, who is being held prisoner on the
enemy planet Drabblova.

Orca Book Publishers gratefully acknowledges the support for its
publishing programs provided by the following agencies:
the Government of Canada through the Book Publishing Industry
Development Program (BPIDP), the Canada Council for the Arts, and
the British Columbia Arts Council.

Layout by Lynn O'Rourke
Cover and interior illustrations by Cindy Revell

**In Canada:**                    **In the United States:**
ORCA BOOK PUBLISHERS              ORCA BOOK PUBLISHERS
Box 5626 Stn.B                   PO Box 468
Victoria, BC  Canada             Custer, WA  USA
v8r 6s4                          98240-0468

08  07 06 05 04 • 6 5 4 3 2 1

Printed and bound in Canada

*To Ian and Ron,*

*my now grown children,
who inspired me to write, and
for the spirit of the child
to bless us all with sunshine.*

*Appreciations to*

*Maggie, Orca Children's Book Editor,
for her wisdom and support, and
my neighbor Emmie, loyal reader
of all my writings and musings.*

—Heather Sander

# Chapter One

It was exactly the same dream. Every night for a whole week, row upon row of parading frogs and duckies floated through my brain. Every morning I woke up in the same place in the dream, scratching my head. All those frogs and duckies were about to tell me something really important. My dream may not have revealed the mystic message of my future, but it kept gnawing at me. Those frogs and duckies reminded me of something, but I couldn't remember what.

That dream was a big departure from the normal me: Robbie Packford, grade six math nerd. I love statistics, especially the National Hockey League, space flight and early man. Some of the

1

other kids in my class, like, for instance, Chris, call me math geek. It's kind of an insult, but not so bad as some I'd heard.

"Robbie, breakfast," Mom called from downstairs. "You're going to be late." Then she called my little sister Mary, alias, the snitch.

I groaned and rolled out of bed. I'm definitely not a morning person. I was still thinking about all those rows and rows of frogs and duckies as I pulled on my T-shirt and jeans. Then it struck me like a thunderbolt. I started to sweat, not the kind of sweat when you do the morning jogs for the school cross-country practice, but cold sweat, the kind when you know something totally weird is about to happen.

You probably won't believe me when I tell you exactly where that frog and ducky dream came from. You'll probably think I'm nuts. Sometimes even I think I am—nuts, that is. But here's the scoop. All those frogs and duckies I had been dreaming about for the past week were on the pajamas of a scientist called Dr. Freedelhum. It's crazy enough that a grown-up scientist would wear pajamas like those. I mean, I gave up my space pj's in grade four. But the really crazy part was that the owner of those pj's was an alien from the planet Kerbosky.

I glanced around my room. It looked normal: hockey posters on the walls, blinking computer screen in the corner with those mesmerizing winged toasters floating randomly across it. Just a dream, I said to myself. That's what you get for reading those dream books. It was back to mysteries and early man next week.

But I was still thinking about the whole thing as Mary and I rounded the corner to school. I glanced around the playground. Chris, the class bully, was showing off to his friends. These days he usually left me alone, a truce in the playground wars.

I peered across the playground. The kid I was looking for was no ordinary kid. Sure, his name was Jamie and he was in grade six and he looked normal, you know, two eyes, ears at the side of his head, mouth, nose, all the bits in the right places. There was only one thing different about him. He had returned to his home, Kerbosky, after only a few days at our school.

I was the only one in Clover Elementary who knew that Kerbosky wasn't just a little town that no one had ever heard of. Kerbosky was a planet in another galaxy.

Jamie and Dr. Freedelhum (the pj's guy) had beamed me down from their spaceship and had taken off for Kerbosky. And I hadn't seen them since. It seemed like a long time ago, another lifetime, even though it had only been a couple of months. It was all so crazy that I tried not to think about it. I had begun to wonder if it had all been a dream. Even when I opened my secrets box and took out my silent dog whistle and my hockey cards, including Wayne Gretzky—Rookie Year, and held Kerbosky's Medal of Honor in my hands, I still thought I had made it all up.

It was all a dream, Robbie, I said to myself as I stared at the yellow squiggles on the red metal. There are no aliens. You did not whiz through hyperspace with Dr. Freedelhum and Jamie. And the part about the frogs and duckies, it's all in your imagination. Mom is always saying that. Dad too.

Even Mrs. Cardwell my grade six teacher says, "You've got a lively imagination, Robbie Packford." But when she says it, she's not smiling, and her gray eyes are looking right through me. That's when I start to shiver because I'm probably in for the Big T: Trouble.

I wandered around the playground until the bell went, keeping away from Chris and company. Mary had gone off to play with her bratty friends. They were into skipping these days. I walked across the grass. I could have done a couple of laps for cross-country, but I wandered in behind the music portable instead.

I jumped when I heard it. "Psst," someone said in a stage whisper. "Robbie, over here."

I looked around. I couldn't see anyone on the grass or behind the portable. But that whisper sounded familiar. Even though it was a warm spring morning, I shivered.

"Up here," whispered the voice. I looked up into the great Garry oak. Climbing the Garry oak in the school yard was a big no, no. It was a heritage tree from the time when only First Nations people lived here. Being up in it meant

5

an instant lecture from the principal, plus several lunch hours of garbage duty.

"Up here," said the voice again. I squinted through the sunlight and the spring leaves. My jaw dropped.

"It's me, Jamie," said the voice, and the boy in the tree, who was about my size except with reddish brown hair instead of dirty blond and hazel eyes instead of blue, waved at me. He smiled and beckoned me to come closer to the gnarled trunk of the old oak.

"I'm back," he said.

# Chapter Two

At that instant the bell rang. I hesitated. Maybe I was finally having one of those lucid dreams like in the book. Jamie sure did look real, though, exactly how I remembered him when he had first come to school. First, Jamie's formula turned me into a monster that noshed down on raw meat. Then there was the spaceship part, and the four billion robots poised to take over the universe.

I pinched myself.

"Ouch," I yelled. I felt awake.

I kept squinting up at the boy in the Garry oak. I was thinking that I'd have to go down to the callback program to tell them that I was late.

While I was thinking, Jamie slithered down the trunk of the tree.

"You're not real, right?" I said. "I know I'm dreaming you. It's time for me to wake up and get into school." The school yard had emptied. Even the few stragglers from the basketball court had gathered up their ball and disappeared through the big double doors. The school yard was silent.

Jamie clapped me on the arm. "Of course you're not dreaming, Robbie," he said. "I beamed down a few minutes ago. I figured you'd be along to school, so I was waiting."

I touched the sleeve of Jamie's jacket. It felt like real cloth.

"Are you going to be in Mrs. Cardwell's class again?" I asked. "Maybe we could be partners in the science fair."

Jamie shook his head. "I've got my own school in Kerbosky," he said. "I even have a private robot tutor."

"You just dropped in for a visit from another galaxy?" I asked.

"Yes and no," answered Jamie.

"Yes and no?" I repeated.

When Jamie smiled I remembered how much I had liked him as a friend even though he had only been at Clover Elementary for a few days. I had missed him.

"I'm glad to see you," he said, "and we need your help."

"We?"

Jamie nodded. "Dr. Freedelhum and I. There is a bit of a crisis on Kerbosky. The president's been kidnapped."

I remembered the president of Kerbosky. He had presented me with the medal that was now in my secrets box. He had seemed more interested in pizza than in me.

"He's being held for ransom in suspended animation," Jamie continued, "and time is running out to save him."

I thought about turning away, sauntering into school, reporting to the callback program, taking my seat in Mrs. Cardwell's class and getting out my spelling book. We always did spelling first thing. I could pretend that this was just another bad dream. But one look at Jamie changed my mind. He had sure been a better friend to me than Chris and Darryl and the other guys who teased me. Jamie had always been on my side. Maybe he and Dr. Freedelhum were a little strange, but they had never been mean to me, not once.

"How can I help?" I asked. "The only thing I know about the president is that he likes pizza."

"That," cried Jamie, "is the whole problem."

## Chapter Three

"You want something from the automatic molecular food processor?" Jamie asked.

We were back on the tiny spaceship. Dr. Freedelhum had beamed us up. A sapphire blue light had enveloped us and our molecules had shimmered and disappeared and all trace of Robbie Packford had left the Clover Elementary schoolyard. Robbie Packford was AWOL.

The callback parent would be asking where I was. No one would believe that I was in an alien spaceship orbiting Earth's moon.

I glanced around the spaceship control room. It looked like a movie set with blinking computer consoles, even a groovy captain's chair that could sit up, lie down, contour itself to your body and probably throw you on the floor with the push of a button. Jamie handed me a tiny object that looked halfway between an earring and a golden button. I remembered. I put the object in my ear, despite what Mom always says about the dangers of putting foreign objects in ears. It melted into my skin. This little baby was a universal translator. Now I would be able to speak, read and understand every known language in the universe. I stared at the squiggles on the computer screens. Some of them had turned into words, but I still couldn't understand what they meant. I wondered if the Kerboskians had come up with instabrains yet. An instabrain sure would help my lagging socials project back on Earth.

Dr. Freedelhum was smiling at me. His kinky curly white hair sprang out from the top of his head. His pince-nez wiggled on the end of his long nose and his lab coat looked more white and starched than ever. I wondered if he still had the frog and ducky pajamas.

"You could order pizza," said Jamie. "The automatic food processor has more Earth varieties than ever." Jamie's voice had gone very quiet when he said these words.

I shook my head. "Just finished breakfast," I said.

At the mention of pizza, Dr. Freedelhum turned a little green. He whimpered. His last words before I had beamed back to Earth last time were, "Thanks for the pizza, Robbie. It's a great contribution to Kerboskian civilization." Now he wasn't ordering one at all, let alone saying, "Make mine with everything."

He stared into my face. "Robbie, my boy," he said, "pizza is the root of all evil."

I opened my mouth, but no words came out. Lots of things could be evil—war, allowing starvation to happen, even not recycling—but pizza? That was going a little too far.

"The Kerboskians loved pizza," I exploded at last. "They had the biggest pizza party ever, every kind ever invented on Earth, after Kerbosky was saved from the robots."

Dr. Freedelhum nodded. "Yes," he said, "it is

all the rage on Kerbosky. Everyone wants pizza, more and more pizza. It's become addictive. The whole planet is mad for pizza."

"What does that have to do with the president?" I demanded. "Jamie says he's been kidnapped."

"And held for ransom," Jamie added.

"All because of pizza," said Dr Freedelhum, peering at me with his red-rimmed eyes. "One taste and a Kerboskian is addicted forever."

"I don't understand," I said, and I didn't.

Dr. Freedelhum blew his nose loudly into a handkerchief. I looked closely at it. Did his handkerchief have frogs and duckies on it too?

"Jamie, you explain the whole sorry problem to our friend. I need a rest."

With that Dr. Freedelhum stood up and fiddled with the orbit controls. He shook his head and his pince-nez wavered on the end of his nose. "I always thought Earth was rather a nice friendly sort of planet," he said sadly to himself.

"Wake me up when we're ready for the hyperspace jump," he said to Jamie and disappeared into his cabin.

I stared at Jamie. Dr. Freedelhum was not himself. Jamie shook his head. "Bad case of pizza withdrawal."

"What?" I said.

Jamie nodded. "I hope he doesn't get the shakes. It was bad enough for me. I never want to see pizza again as long as I live."

I was still staring. "You were addicted to pizza?"

Jamie nodded. "It was bad, Robbie, really bad. I couldn't think of anything but pizza for days: Hawaiian pizza, house pizza, even plain pizza with tomato sauce and mozzarella. No need for double pepperoni. Just more and more pizza. Breakfast. Lunch. Dinner. Midnight snack. All of Kerbosky was like that. Most still are. Kerbosky is a mess!"

"But what does that have to do with the president?" I demanded again. "You still haven't told me why he was kidnapped."

"I was coming to that," Jamie said. "It had to do with the patent and the franchise."

"The patent and the what?" I replied.

"When the president and his council saw what

a hit pizza was, they patented the computer program and franchised the right to make Earth pizza. That was before we cottoned on to the addicting part."

"You mean the president and his pals were making a fortune out of pizza?" I asked.

Jamie nodded.

"But everyone on Earth knows about pizza," I said. "We've got six billion people on earth. Probably about one billion of them ate pizza in the last week, and even I could tell you all the ingredients and I'm only eleven years old."

"But that's on Earth," Jamie said. "On Kerbosky, the pizza recipe is a big secret. Nobody knows how to cook. They program what they want into the automatic molecular food processor. He who controls pizza controls Kerbosky. They'd do anything for pizza down there. They'd practically sell their own grandmothers for a large with triple pepperoni."

I gasped. The chances of this happening must be about—I didn't even want to think about it.

"Okay, Jamie, let me get this straight," I said.

"Everyone on Kerbosky is addicted to pizza except you because somehow you got over the craving."

"And it sure was hard," Jamie admitted. "I had it bad, the pizza craving. I wondered if I'd make it."

I nodded. "But you're okay now." Jamie scrunched up his face, remembering, but he looked the same as ever to me so I continued. "And the president was making a killing off the rights to sell pizza." Jamie kept on nodding. "Then someone else thought it was a great scheme, but they needed the secret computer formula so they kidnapped the president and won't let him go until Kerbosky gives them the formula."

"Correct," Jamie said. "And he's in suspended animation until the kidnappers hear from the Kerboskian Council."

"Why don't you just give them the formula?" I demanded. "It's no big deal."

Jamie nodded again. "At first, the council were getting so rich they thought they could just replace the president; then they noticed that everyone was getting addicted. Kerboskians would do anything for pizza. Remember how mean the robots were when the Master Ordinance got changed? That's nothing compared to Kerboskians now. Imagine what it would be like on Earth if every single person only wanted to eat pizza all day long. When there was none left they'd start getting jumpy. Then downright mean. Supposing someone could control all that?"

I scratched my ear. "I see what you mean. And I suppose the kidnappers are some pretty bad dudes."

"Now you've got it all figured out," exclaimed Jamie. "Once the kidnappers have the secret formula, that's it for Kerbosky."

"Who exactly are these kidnappers?" I asked at last. "And how are you going to get the president out of this mess?"

I was breathing more heavily. If everyone on Kerbosky was addicted to pizza and Dr. Freedelhum was going through pizza withdrawal, then the only one who could save the president and the planet was Jamie. I didn't see anyone else on the spaceship. And Jamie only had one friend to help him against a bunch of kidnappers and a planet full of crazy pizza addicts. I was having some bad feelings about what Jamie was going to say next.

Of course, he went right ahead and said it. "It's up to us, Robbie," he whispered. "We are the only ones who can save Kerbosky."

# Chapter Four

Dr. Freedelhum stared at the automatic molecular food processor. His eyes were vacant and his pince-nez wobbled. Jamie was readjusting our orbit around the moon. We were supposed to be making a plan to get the president back and save Kerboksy. Jamie thought that I could help with the addiction part. How was it that Kerboskians got addicted, but Earthlings didn't?

I should have gone into school when the bell went, I thought. I would be in math class right now, the only place where I really shone. Even Chris wanted to be my math partner. Otherwise he ignored me unless he had thought up an extra special insult.

"There," said Jamie, "the spaceship is on automatic pilot. We don't have much time."

While Jamie had been working the controls, Dr. Freedelhum had been inching across the chamber. He glanced at Jamie to see if he was watching. Then his body kind of slithered towards the food processor. I didn't like the glazed-over look in his rabbit-like eyes. A drip of saliva was forming in the corner of his mouth. His pink tongue darted over his lips and he wiped his face with yet another frog and ducky handkerchief.

When Dr. Freedelhum came to Earth the first time, he thought that Earth fashion meant frog and ducky pj's and the pince-nez. So much for Kerboskian research. I glanced back and forth between the two aliens. This was not a good start to operation "Save the President."

I gazed into Dr. Freedelhum's glistening eyes with their purply pinkish glow. That was another thing about Kerboskians: though they looked a lot like humans, one thing was very different about them—their eyes. Kerboskian eyes are various shades of pink and purple. Jamie didn't want to scare me or my friends on the Clover Elementary playground so he had altered his eye color. Dr. Freedelhum had too, but he hadn't covered up all the telltale pinks and purples.

It was amazing what Kerboskian technology could do. They used special contact lenses, but there was something else about electromagnetism and molecular rearrangement that I couldn't get my brain around. No matter how you cut it, Kerboskians were different from Earthlings. Not like someone from another country moving in down the street. Kerbosky was so many galaxies away from Earth that our telescopes weren't powerful enough to pick up even a hint of their solar system.

I was still staring at Dr. Freedelhum. I didn't want to rat on him, but even I could tell that he was in the grips of pizzamania. His shaking hand was only inches from the automatic molecular food processor. His tongue was darting out of his mouth like a lizard's. His eyes looked crazed. "Make mine with everything," he whispered over and over again.

Jamie turned around. Dr. Freedelhum froze. "Dr. Freedelhum!" Jamie cried out. "You must be strong. You can't give in to the craving now."

"Just one bite," the doctor whimpered. "I'll cut down gradually. First I'll cut out olives, then peppers. Soon I'll be down to plain cheese and tomato sauce. It will be easy after that."

Jamie shook his head. "Dr. Freedelhum, you must be strong," he said again. "Kerbosky is depending on you."

Large tears spilled over from Dr. Freedelhum's eyes. He blew his nose into the frogs and duckies. "I can't stand it," he moaned. "I'd do anything for one bite of pizza with everything."

It was pathetic. A grown scientist was whining about pizza. Dr. Freedelhum was worse than useless. He was a liability. I stared at Jamie and he stared at me. We both gulped. It was up to us to save the president. I wished I'd never heard of pizza.

Jamie stepped between the automatic molecular food processor and Dr. Freedelhum's shaking hand. "It will be okay soon," he said, but I could hear the doubt in his voice. "Why not have a rest? Robbie will bring you some warm milk."

Dr. Freedelhum kept whimpering, but more quietly. Like a mantra, he repeated, "Make mine with everything."

"I think you should go to your cabin," Jamie said.

Dr. Freedelhum sighed and nodded. "Can you bring me my teddy?" he asked.

"Yes," Jamie said. He turned to me. "It started with pizza. Then Kerboksy had this Earth craze. Earth stuffed toys are a big item. Dr. Freedelhum is inseparable from his. You can put on your frog and ducky pajamas," he told Dr. Freedelhum. "They always make you feel better."

Dr. Freedelhum clapped his hands together. He almost smiled. I was beginning to think that this was one of the worst performances I had ever seen. "Dial up some warm milk on the automatic molecular processor," Jamie said to me. "I'll help Dr. Freedelhum into his pj's."

I dialed up warm milk on the computer console, just like Robbie had shown me. The door of the processor slid open, and I picked up the tray with the steaming milk on it. Ugh. At least the doctor could have ordered hot chocolate. Bleahh!

Dr. Freedelhum was already in his frog and ducky pj's when I entered his cabin. I looked at his bed. His pillow had duckies on it and the sheet that Robbie was tucking around him had dozens of frogs on it, each with their tongues stretched out, straining to catch a fly that hovered just above their bulging eyes. The cabin was green with lily pads all over the walls. I hated to think of what his underwear might look like.

"Warm milk, as ordered," I said, passing the glass to Jamie.

He pressed it into Dr. Freedelhum's hand. "Drink up, doctor," he said, "and get some rest."

In between slurps, Dr. Freedelhum whispered to himself. "Make mine with everything. Pleeee-aase, make mine with everything."

"It's a bad case," Jamie said, pressing the control to close the cabin door. "Dr. Freedelhum might be this way for some time."

"And no help to us," I added.

Jamie nodded. "We'd better program in a

lock on the computer console. Dr. Freedel-hum might get up in the middle of the night and try to order pizza. One bite and he'd have to start the pizza decontamination process all over again."

"How could this happen?" I demanded. "The chances of your species being addicted to pizza must be…"

"Four hundred and ninety-nine trillion, three hundred and sixty-two million, one hundred thousand and four to one," finished Jamie. "I worked it out." Jamie held out a shiny flat disk. "If you stick this on your forehead, the computer will download your specs."

"What?" I asked, eyeing the little disk.

"Just to give us more info about your earth physiology, DNA, stuff like that. Maybe we can prevent the whole planet of Kerbosky from going through pizza withdrawal. You eat pizza all the time, no problem. Right?" I nodded, still staring at the disk. "It will only take a moment and you won't feel a thing."

"Okay," I said doubtfully, sticking the disk in the middle of my forehead.

Jamie fiddled with some buttons on the computer. "Downloading in progress. This part is easy. It's the analysis and comparison with Kerboskians that takes time: time we don't have right now. We have to get busy and make our plan." Jamie plucked the disc off my forehead. He was right. I hadn't felt a thing. He looked away. "They might be after us already," he said.

There were two things that I didn't like about what Jamie had just said. One was this "we" business. There was no one else around to help. Then there was the "they" business. "Who exactly are the 'they' who might be after us already?" I asked.

"The president's kidnappers, of course," Jamie said.

"Are they like a gang or something?" I asked, thinking of the mafia.

"Kind of," replied Jamie.

"I suppose they're pretty mean and nasty," I said, with a sinking feeling in the pit of my stomach.

Jamie nodded. He scratched his head. "We'll have to look like them to penetrate their hide-out," he said.

"You mean, wear a disguise," I said, thinking this was getting to be like a spy movie. Jamie nodded again. "What kind of disguise?" I asked.

Jamie was deep in thought. "Maybe we could program the automatic molecular food processor to make the parts we need."

"Parts?" This disguise bit was sounding stranger and stranger.

"Hmm," said Jamie, ignoring my question. "We could program the extra fingers and even the extra eye."

"What?" I shrieked. "The kidnappers have extra fingers and a third eye? I suppose their internal organs are in different places too."

Jamie nodded again. "That part doesn't matter because they can't see inside us."

I grabbed Jamie and began to shake him. "This is nuts," I shouted. "What else aren't you telling me?"

Jamie frowned. "Oh," he said, "I guess I did forget to tell you that part. The president's kidnappers aren't from Kerbosky. They're from the planet Drabblova."

# Chapter Five

Jamie had been fiddling with the keyboard on the computer for a long time. He hummed tunelessly to himself. I was getting hungry, but I didn't want to interrupt him. The only things I knew how to dial up on the automatic food processor were hot milk and pizza. Somehow, I didn't think either was a good idea.

"At last!" exclaimed Jamie. "I've got it! While I program the computer for our—er—spare parts, I'll tell you about Drabblova."

"Okay," I answered doubtfully. Was this going to be something I really wanted to hear? I thought not, but knowing Jamie I was going to hear it anyhow. And then I was going to find out the bad part, like some crazy scheme that wouldn't work without my help.

"You know how we have two suns on Kerbosky?" Jamie asked. I nodded. That part would have been hard to forget. Try to find a shady spot to relax on a planet with two suns shining down on you from different parts of the sky. "Well," continued Jamie, "suns aren't the only thing we have two of. We have two planets too."

Two planets, I thought. Well, old Sol back in the Milky Way had nine planets revolving around it. Of course, only one, as far as we knew, had ever been inhabited except when they thought all those lines on Mars were canals dug by an advanced civilization. It turned out to be totally untrue, of course. So Kerbosky's system had two suns and two inhabited planets.

"Just imagine," said Jamie, "if your moon were much bigger, say about the size of Earth."

"You mean," I said, "Kerbosky has a twin planet? Two Kerboskys?"

Jamie shrugged. "Not like identical twins," he said. "Kerbosky and Drabblova aren't at all alike." Here Jamie stopped. I was certain that

I wasn't going to like the next part. "Well," he went on, "even though Kerbosky and Drabblova have complicated intersecting orbits, Kerboskians and Drabblovians don't exactly get along."

A shiver went down my back. "The two planets hate each other, don't they?" I said. "And it's a bit more serious than the Toronto Maple Leafs versus the Montreal Canadians, isn't it?"

"You got it!" Jamie said. "They want everything we have and we want everything they have."

"And now they have the chance to control all of Kerbosky by keeping you addicted to pizza."

"That's it in a nutshell," Jamie admitted, pushing the last command in the computer program. The door of the automatic molecular food processor slid open and Jamie reached in. "Hold out your hand," he said.

"Tell me this isn't going to hurt," I said.

"This part won't hurt, Robbie. The only part that's going to hurt is if the Drabblovians find out we're really from Kerbosky."

The shivers continued up and down my spine. "Or from Earth," I corrected.

"Right," said Jamie. "The Drabblovians don't like anyone much. Let me see if this fits your hand. I think I've got the specifications right."

I stared. Jamie was holding a finger and smiling. My stomach lurched. It looked exactly like a finger that had been taken off someone's hand. I gagged. The only good part was that there was no blood spurting out of it. That would have been the end of me. Jamie already had my hand in his. I wanted to yell, "Wait, I haven't agreed to this!", but he was already grinning all over.

"Perfect!" he said. "It matches your molecular configuration perfectly. You'd never know you weren't born this way." I stared at my hand. It still felt like my hand. I curled my fingers into a ball. It still worked like my hand. But it had an extra baby finger tacked on at the end. When I waved my hand, the extra finger waved too, as if it had always belonged to me.

"Now your other hand," said Jamie, holding out another finger. "That didn't hurt one bit, did it?"

I shook my head and rubbed my hand over the extra finger. It felt warm. "Will it drop off?" I asked.

Jamie shook his head as he attached the other one. "Not until we change the computer program," he answered. "Next we'll do the extra eye. It's a little trickier, but I've got the program worked out."

If you think seeing an extra finger or two lying around is a little sickening, wait until you see an eyeball pop out of an automatic molecular processor. Not only that, the thing blinked at me.

"No," I said firmly. "I'm not having that gross thing in the middle of my forehead. I like me the way I am. I can see perfectly well with only two eyes."

It was too late. Jamie was already plugging the extra eye into my forehead. He hummed tunelessly as he worked. I was already on an alien spaceship. Now I was turning into an alien. Jamie produced a mirror. "Very fashionable," he said, "for a Drabblovian."

I blinked. I gasped. All three of my eyes blinked back at me from the mirror. My middle eyeball

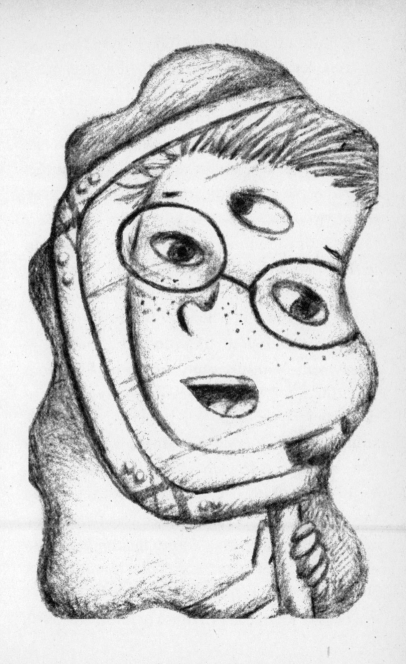

rolled around in its socket like it was trying to look at my two original eyes. I felt seasick. I groaned.

"It's okay," Jamie said. "You just need a little practice coordinating three eyes. Look to the right and the left and back again, trying to get your middle eye to do the same thing as your other two eyes. Take the mirror."

I practiced, but my new eye refused to cooperate. It wandered around randomly inside its socket. I was getting dizzier by the minute. You know how you feel when you've made yourself go cross-eyed about fifty times by looking at your nose? Multiply that by about a thousand, and you'll know exactly how I was feeling.

I was just about to tell Jamie this third eye thing would never work when he tapped me on the shoulder. "How do I look?" he asked.

All three of my eyes stopped dead and stared out of my forehead. Jamie now had three eyes. His third eyeball was rolling up and down and around and around in its socket while the other two stood still. It looked gross.

"I think we both need more practice," he said,

looking at himself in the mirror. "I've got the finger thing down, but I hadn't predicted how tricky the eye part was going to be."

Jamie admired himself in the mirror while he worked on coordinating his third eye with the others. "Don't worry," he said at last. "We've got time to practice on the way to Drabblova. And I'll explain our plan to you."

"Plan?" I echoed, trying to get my third eye to stop spinning around.

Jamie nodded. He was already at the computer pulling us out of our orbit around Earth's moon. "Our plan to infiltrate Drabblova, free the president and rid Kerbosky forever of the dread of pizza."

My mouth opened to protest, but the spaceship had already jumped into hyperspace. With each beat of my heart the distance between me and the playground at Clover Elementary was increasing by millions of kilometers.

# Chapter Six

Jamie was right. Practice helped. All three of my eyes were now working together most of the time and only sudden movements made me seasick. The two new fingers worked as if they had been there forever. I was even getting used to the look of my six-fingered hands. What if all Earthlings had six fingers? Base ten would be out. We could keep old-fashioned rulers with twelve inches because twelve is two times six.

"Planning time," Jamie said. "We'll be entering the Kerboskian system in a few hours. By then we need everything down pat."

I wiggled all my fingers and rolled all my eyes. "Down pat?" I shouted. My six fingers grabbed

Jamie's arm. "How can we get a plan down pat when we don't have any plan at all?"

Jamie looked at his watch. "We've only got three hours and six minutes before we go into orbit around Drabblova. Let's not waste time."

"I need something to eat if we're going to make up a plan to take on a whole planet," I said, stalling.

Jamie nodded. "But no pizza!" he said. "Now even the smell of it makes me feel sick."

Just as well, I thought, all things considered. We munched on burgers and fries and chocolate milk. Even salad. Jamie had taken a fancy to spinach, having begun a study of Earth comic books and discovering Popeye.

"I think he got his out of a can," I said, thinking spinach salad wasn't so bad. "But spinach is not going to make you extra strong. Comic books are just make-believe."

Jamie looked disappointed. What was I saying? There I was eating spinach salad in a spaceship getting ready to invade an alien planet and I was talking about make-believe!

Jamie had pulled up a map of Drabblova on the computer. The planet showed up in 3D. It sailed through space in miniature. Clouds formed and reformed on its surface. They were whitish like ours, but the planet itself didn't look a bit like those photos of Earth from space, our good old blue marble. Drabblova looked a little sick, kind of yellowy, and the sky had a pinky sort of glow.

"It's the refraction of the light from the two suns. It makes our sky yellow and the Drabblovian sky pink. Plus Drabblovia always has this slight haze in the atmosphere, more refraction, red spectrum," Jamie explained. "No problem once you get used to it." He fiddled with the control panel. "I can zoom in on any part of the planet." The computer screen gave a jump in front of my eyes. It was like I was falling from the sky at an alarming rate. I gasped.

"Optical illusion," Jamie said as he worked the console. Apparently, with six fingers you could type commands even faster than with five. Now we were diving into a city. Orange and pink and blue buildings rushed up at us at dizzying speed. Jamie chattered away. "Capital city of Drabblova, Quintisseblum. Never did like their color scheme. Ah, here's the main government building and the Drabblovian president's office. This is where I think our president is being held."

"Can't you tell for sure?" I asked, squinting at the screen.

"Wish I could. Our technology isn't good enough to penetrate the force field around their presidential quarters, but we'll teleport ourselves into the heart of the city. Then we just walk right into the government building and the president's office. See?" With the push of a button a floor plan of the whole building rolled off the printer. The president's office was highlighted in red. The nifty computer program had already marked out the best route.

I stared at the map. "Wouldn't there be the small matter of guards? On Earth you can't just walk into some world leader's office and say, 'Hi.' You'd get arrested."

Jamie nodded. "You're right," he said. "We'll have to sneak in."

I groaned. Jamie did not have a plan at all. He just had a fancy computer that made cute maps. He had no idea how to get past the president's security system. Old spy movies flashed before my eyes. We weren't strong enough to overpower the guards. That was out. We could dress up as repairmen, waiters, manufacture guard uniforms in the molecular processor. Any of the above. How did I know?

"We could dress up as repairmen or waiters or even guards," said Jamie. Was he reading my mind? "We could make the uniforms in the automatic molecular processor."

Jamie's fingers flew over the control panel and the *Encyclopedia of Drabblova* appeared, *Thirty-ninth Edition*. Jamie scrolled up and down revealing a dazzling array of Drabblovian clothes. They seemed to go in for pink.

"Ugh," I said.

Jamie shrugged. "What's your choice, presidential guard, presidential waiter? Here's the food taster's uniform. Next to the president, food tasters are the most important people on the planet. But their careers are kind of short. All

Drabblovians are afraid of being poisoned."

"Poisoned?" I shuddered.

Jamie nodded. "I forgot to tell you that part about Drabblova. That's how you get to be president. You have to poison the old president and then it's your turn until..."

"Until?" I echoed.

"Until you get poisoned too, of course. The average time in office is...Let's see." Jamie scrolled up the computer. "Seventy-four days. Their record is three presidents in one day."

Great, I thought, we were going to a planet of poisoners who wanted to enslave their neighboring planet to pizza. "This is too crazy," I whispered to myself over and over. I was beginning to feel like Dr. Freedelhum.

"And one other thing," Jamie said.

I don't want to hear this, I thought. But Jamie went ahead and told me anyway. "Drabblovian food is some of the worst in the entire universe. If they offer you some, say you've just eaten."

# Chapter Seven

Behind us, a voice whimpered, "They're fighting again. I can't stop them."

Jamie and I spun around. Dr. Freedelhum was still in his frog and ducky pajamas. His hands shook. His pince-nez quivered. A large tear wobbled in the corner of each eye. He looked about to cry. But that wasn't the strangest part.

Dr. Freedelhum was holding a stuffed animal in each outstretched hand. They DID look like they had had a fight. In his right hand was a raggedy teddy bear with a large rip in its fur. Stuffing was oozing out of the tear. A button eye hung by a thread. Teddy was bedraggled and wet. In my opinion, the stuffed frog had gotten the best of the contest. It had only a few small tears and had lost no stuffing from its plump green body. Its tiny black beady eyes gave it a mean expression. Its long frog legs dangled limply from Dr. Freedelhum's hand. "Froggy tried to drown Teddy in the swamp," the doctor said.

"What?" Jamie and I demanded together.

Now Dr. Freedelhum was really crying. "Poor Teddy," he whispered. "Froggy almost put an end to him. It was all about pizza."

Jamie took the soaking teddy. "It's okay," he said, patting Dr. Freedelhum's arm. He turned to me. "It's pizzamania, Robbie. I've seen it before. Dr. Freedelhum thinks his toys are real. He thinks they're giving him messages about pizza."

Dr. Freedelhum was pressing the mean little frog into my hands. "You have to reason with him, Robbie," he whimpered. "I can't get him to stop hurting Teddy."

I took the frog. Much more of this and I'd be talking to stuffed animals myself.

"You'd better sit down, doctor," said Jamie. "Robbie, more warm milk from the automatic molecular food processor, please. It will calm him until this fit passes."

While I fiddled with the computer, Dr. Freedelhum told us more about the war between the stuffed toys.

"Teddy wouldn't stop talking," he said.

"What was he saying?" asked Jamie.

"'Make mine with everything,' over and over. Froggy couldn't stand it anymore."

Jamie nodded. "I thought as much," he said. "The last stage of pizzamania is the worst. You just have to get through this, Dr. Freedlehum, and you'll be back to normal. Froggy just wants to help."

"But he doesn't have to get so angry," Dr. Freedelhum said. "Look at what he did to Teddy."

Jamie turned to me. "The two parts of Dr. Freedelhum are fighting it out inside of him. He believes the stuffed animals are doing it."

I nodded. I must be going crazy myself, I thought. This was starting to sound normal.

"Poor Teddy," cried Dr. Freedelhum. "Look at what mean Froggy did to his little button eyes. He used to be so cute."

"They'll get along again," promised Jamie, "just as soon as you're better."

The doctor's eyes narrowed. "One little bite of pizza would make me better right now," he said. "Any kind of pizza would do, Mexican, pizza with Canadian bacon, Hawaiian—"

Jamie shook his head. "Be patient, Dr. Freedelhum," he said. "Soon you'll be fine. In the meantime, let's fix Teddy in the molecular processor."

Dr. Freedelhum nodded, still whimpering. Jamie placed the bear in the computer, and I gave Dr. Freedelhum his warm milk. In seconds Teddy was as good as new. His little bear face smiled brightly as Dr. Freedelhum hugged him and rocked him. Of course, ten minutes before he had smiled brightly while he was having the stuffing knocked out of him.

"Now," Jamie said sternly, "we are in orbit around Drabblova. We only need you to do one thing, Dr. Freedelhum." Dr. Freedelhum rocked and rocked. "Robbie and I have to go down to the planet's surface to rescue the president of Kerbosky. We need you to work the teleporter. I've already programmed the coordinates. You just have to press the button. And when we're ready to return, we'll call you on the communication device and you press the button to bring us back. Do you think you can do that?"

Dr. Freedelhum nodded and rocked, rocked and nodded. "Nasty Froggy won't hurt you anymore, dear Teddy," he crooned.

"Dr. Freedelhum," Jamie said again, "we have to save the president. This is the last chance for Kerbosky. Can you do it for our planet? Can you be strong?"

Dr. Freedelhum nodded. "I know what I have to do," he said tearfully. How could Jamie trust Dr. Freedelhum, I wondered. Sure, all he had to do was press a button at the right time and wait for our message, but what if he couldn't? We would be trapped with a whole planet of angry Drabblovians and their gross food forever.

"He'll be okay, I promise," said Jamie, but none of his three eyes met mine.

Jamie turned back to the control panel. "In three minutes we will be passing above the capital city of Drabblova. I can put us down right in the main square outside of the presidential complex. Let's check out our equipment."

I nodded, feeling dazed. We were putting our lives in the hand of someone who thought stuffed toys talked to him. "Universal translator," said Jamie.

"Check," I said touching the tiny gold earring that allowed me to understand, speak and read all the known languages in the universe.

"Communications device."

"Check," I said, touching the miniature transmitter in my utility belt which would allow us to talk to Dr. Freedelhum back on the spaceship. If he was listening.

"Drabblovian presidential guard uniform."

"Check," I said, clapping my hand against my chest in the Drabblovian salute that Jamie had taught me. I looked in the mirror. Drabblovian tastes were pretty weird. If I wore this uniform to school, I'd be laughed out of grade six. Shocking pink and slimy lime were despicable colors. No one in their right mind would have chosen those colors for a uniform on Earth, but Earth was far away, several galaxies away, as a matter of fact.

"Poison pellets," said Jamie.

"What!"

"That little green package in your utility belt. Don't touch them. They're deadly."

I glanced at the small green package dangling from my utility belt. "They're next to the bombs, the white capsules."

"Bombs!" I gazed at the white capsules stuck in the belt like bullets.

"Don't touch them either. They're stink bombs, actually. One whiff and a whole spaceship full of people would pass out." Great, I thought. Not only did Drabblovians eat gross food and have no taste in clothes and poison each other just for fun, they attacked each other with stink bombs.

Jamie edged us towards the teleporter. "Let me do the talking," he said. "I understand Drabblovian customs."

I nodded. I didn't want to talk to the Drabblovians. I would have preferred not meeting them at all.

Was it too late to ask if I could be sent back to Earth?

Dr. Freedelhum was already fiddling with the teleporter controls. I felt myself beginning to fade out. Dr. Freedelhum was making the teleporter work just as Jamie had asked, but he was making Teddy wave bye-bye to us at the same time. Dr. Freedelhum was mouthing the words, "Make mine with everything."

"No!" I shouted. "This is not going to work."

It was too late. The blue light of the teleporter had enveloped us and my atoms shimmered and began to fade into nothingness. The sickening pink and lime of Jamie's Drabblovian uniform faded out. His smile stayed behind for a moment like the Cheshire cat's in *Alice in Wonderland*. Then...nothing.

# Chapter Eight

I blinked. I stared. I think my mouth gaped open. My eyes hurt. Jamie pushed me into the tiny shadow cast by a building under two suns. He handed me a pair of sunglasses. "Everyone on Drabblova wears these," he explained. "Their orbit takes them a bit closer to our suns than Kerbosky's orbit does."

"Ah," I said, putting on the sunglasses. They were the only cool thing about Drabblova so far. Sweat was already dripping down inside the disgusting slime green and shocking pink uniform.

But the colors I was wearing had nothing on the general color scheme of the whole place. A riot of multicolored buildings surrounded us: greens and purples, plaids, bright yellows, every shade you could imagine. People walked across the square. They smiled. They waved their six fingers at each other. They looked around with their three eyes, which all seemed to work in unison. Their clothes were iridescent shades of everything. You know those TV shows of tropical seas where you see all those exquisite multicolored fish? They paled in comparison to Drabblova. If the suns hadn't already hurt my eyes, Drabblovian clothes would have.

"Stand up straight," Robbie ordered. "You're slumping. Remember, you have to look like a guard." I nodded, still sweating from the heat and from worry. I couldn't imagine anyone believing that we were presidential guards. "Let me do the talking, and whatever you do, don't accept any Drabblovian food."

I nodded again and straightened my shoulders, wondering if we would have to poison any people to get into the president's office. I had been in trouble in the playground a few times—once for rough play, once for swearing—but I had never even gotten close to poisoning anyone, unless you count the time I made a Mother's Day cake and got the salt mixed up with the sugar. I thought of Dr. Freedelhum back on the spaceship and Teddy's little paw waving bye-bye. I wondered if Teddy and Froggy were fighting again, or worse, if Dr. Freedelhum was busy programming up pizza with everything, in which case he would have forgotten us altogether. "How do you know Dr. Freedelhum is doing his job up there?" I asked, looking up into the bright sky.

Jamie shrugged. "It's like this, Robbie," he said, "sometimes you have to trust." I must have looked miserable because he added, "But I did put a lock on the programmer so it won't make pizza. Dr. Freedelhum could reprogram it, but it would take a long time."

I imagined Dr. Freedelhum at the computer console pressing buttons feverishly. Teddy would be sitting in his lap, and Dr. Freedelhum, his eyes glinting, would be whispering, "Make mine with everything."

But Jamie was already striding across the square to the largest building of all. I had to crane my neck to see to the top of it, thirty or forty stories up. Each floor was a different color, starting with earth shades and passing through the whole spectrum to pinks and yellows on top. Now is the time to wake up, I thought. Maybe, if I thought of this as a lucid dream, the kind I read about, a crazy sort of dream, but one you could wake up from… But we were already at the marble steps to the grand building, each step a different hue. Guards, some in slime green and shocking pink, others in iridescent purple and bird's-eye blue, saluted us. I saluted back, just as Jamie had taught me.

The guards looked like they were taking us seriously, at least for now. "I made us high rank- ing," Jamie whispered again. "Just look like you know everything." Right, I thought, like when we had the socials test on ancient Egypt and I forgot to study.

No one stopped us even though we must have looked like a couple of guard midgets. Guards kept saluting, and we were through the gigantic doors into the cool air-conditioned interior. I won't keep telling you about the color scheme inside because it would make your eyes hurt too. Just know that the Drabblovians had every color known on Earth and a few new ones too, but all in one room. Jamie approached a giant escalator and got on as if he had been doing this every day of his life. I followed, still saluting. Guards and other officials hurried everywhere about the building, hundreds on our escalator alone. I was still getting used to the six fingers and the three eyes and was feeling a little sick, but no one paid a bit of attention to us.

The whole operation seemed easy, too easy. I knew how it was. I'd seen the spy movies. There had to be a trap. I listened for movie music in the background—you know, the music that warns you that some monster's about to jump out of the cupboard—but all I could hear was the steady hum of the escalator as it went smoothly up and up, the babble of hundreds of voices and yes, far in the background, even on Drabblova, elevator music.

The main foyer of the building spread out far below, all the colorful people like toys. Up and up we went, past floors and offices and more and more guards and officials until, at last, we reached the top. Jamie stepped off, and I followed, practically crashing into him. He saluted. I saluted. He showed an identification card to another guard. I did too, holding the card with my six fingers. We all saluted again. Maybe this wasn't going to be so bad after all.

Jamie turned to the right. A gleaming corridor stretched before us. Surprisingly, this one was white. All the doors were white. Jamie walked down the corridor towards the end where two guards stood, dressed exactly like us. "This is it," Jamie whispered.

The guards barred the entrance. Jamie saluted. They saluted, but they looked suspicious. This was where our great plan was going to start to fall apart. I felt puny and insignificant. My knees threatened to knock against each other.

"Stand aside," Jamie said, in a very un-Jamie-like voice. "We have an important message for the president."

The guards didn't move. I was sweating again. I could tell they didn't want to let us in.

"Top secret," Jamie whispered. "Life and death, the latest information on the Kerboskian Pizza Mission."

At that, the guards straightened to attention. They talked through the door with a communications device, and at last the great door swung open. More guards to salute. At the far end of a huge room, again white, were a very large desk and a very large overstuffed raised chair. In the overstuffed chair sat what looked like a perfectly round, stuffed man. A large pink mustache drooped under his nose and a pink beard like candy floss grew from his chin. He stared at us through his three eyes.

"Mr. President," said Jamie forcefully, "we have important news for your ears alone about the Kerbosky Pizza Mission. The Kerboskians are about to capitulate."

The president straightened in his chair. He motioned us to come closer. By this time the great door had swung closed behind us, barring all escape. He peered at us and rubbed the six stumpy fingers of each hand together. "At last," he said gleefully, "I will realize my dream.

Those fools will do anything for pizza. Now they will be our slaves forever." Jamie froze at those words, but the president of Drabblova didn't notice. He was too busy laughing. His little round belly shook like a—I won't say a bowl full of jelly, but he did look a little like an evil Santa Claus.

"The Kerboskians have sent their surrender terms, but first they need proof that their president is alive and well," said Jamie. I had to give it to him. That private robot tutor must have made him pretty smart. He sounded just like a character out of a spy movie.

The president of Drabblova kept on laughing. In fact, he had a good case of the giggles. He pounded his desk with glee. He would be rolling on the carpet in another minute. He started to cough and sputter.

"If I may, sir," said Jamie. He stepped forward and clapped the president on the back.

The president gasped for breath. "They're in my power," he said as soon as he could breathe again. "Every single Kerboskian. Now we will get even for everything they have ever done to us."

"The computer formula for pizza—do you have it?" he demanded with a sputter and a burp.

"For the conditions of surrender to be met, I must first determine the physical condition of the president of Kerbosky," said Jamie.

The president of Drabblova nodded. He reached into his desk, pulled out a remote control and pushed a button.

I tried not to gasp. A solid wall suddenly became a transparent window, and behind the window, motionless in his official red uniform with a feathery plumed hat, was the president of Kerbosky. He looked a little plumper than I remembered.

"Too much pizza," Jamie whispered.

When the president of Drabblova looked at the president of Kerbosky behind the glass in suspended animation, it was too much for him. He started to giggle again. "Make mine with everything," he roared with laughter. "That's what they all say."

This was our big chance. Our only chance. Jamie grabbed the remote control from the president's outstretched hand, and we rushed towards the glass. Furiously, Jamie pressed the buttons. The force field evaporated as we rushed forward, and the Kerboskian president blinked. "Did you order out?" he said.

We stared. "For pizza," he wailed. "Where's my pizza?"

"No time for that now, Mr. President," said Jamie. He whispered into the communication device. "Now, Dr. Freedelhum, now. Beam us back RIGHT NOW!" Of course, you know the next part. Absolutely nothing happened. We were not beamed up to the waiting spaceship. Instead, the three of us stood like frozen lumps on the floor. The president of Drabblova was no longer smiling. In fact, he had a real mean look in all of his three eyes.

Guards from all over the room converged on us. They took ugly looking things out of their utility belts, like those white bombs. They pointed weapons at us. Their six fingers curved around the triggers of their atomic blasters. Their three eyes didn't even blink. The end, I thought, goners, and all for a pizza with everything.

## Chapter Nine

"Hit the deck!" shrieked Jamie.

He was pulling an object out of his utility belt, but something told me I didn't want to know what it was. At the same time, he kept yelling uselessly into his communicator, "Beam us up, ppp-lease, Dr. Freedelhum. Beam us up!"

"Can I order out now?" asked the president of Kerbosky.

Then a smell filled the room, not exactly an unpleasant smell. I couldn't quite place it. It wasn't like one of those room fresheners that Mom used when our golden lab Cuddles made, you know, the big smell. I sniffed, trying to place the odor.

I was already on my knees, waiting for Jamie to do whatever it was he was going to do. I just hoped it didn't involve blood and gore. Blood and gore were okay in the movies when you had lots of popcorn to eat and could say to yourself, "Come on, this is only a movie," but real life was different.

The president of Kerbosky had stopped asking us to call the nearest pizza outlet. He had passed out on the floor. Jamie was on his knees, gagging. Some of the guards who had been closing in on us were passing out too. The president of Drabblova wasn't laughing anymore. He wasn't even smiling. His three eyes turned in circles. He turned green and fainted.

The remaining guards had started to turn green too. They all held their breath, dropped their weapons and fished in their utility belts for gas masks. I tried to drag Jamie towards the door. He was like a dead lump, but at least he was still breathing. The heavy odor lingered. It wasn't a scent I would have chosen. Forget the president, I told myself. All he wants is a pizza anyhow.

But it was too late. Guards with gas masks barred our way. They had picked up their weapons again. Some of them were pointed right at my head.

I smiled weakly, trying to look nonchalant. "It's all a mistake," I tried to explain. "They've just fainted. Not to worry."

This didn't help the guards look any friendlier. Every one of their three eyes glared at me without blinking.

"Why didn't you react to the stink bomb?" demanded one.

Think fast, I said to myself. Of course, that meant my brain went completely out of gear and I said my great line, "Maybe I was a little too far away to be affected. I think the captain and I," I pointed to Jamie, still comatose on the floor, "had better be getting along. We have more information gathering to do for the president, you know, top secret." I pulled at Jamie's uniform, but he was still passed out, no use to anyone.

The guards came closer. One of them held an atomic blaster to my forehead. "You are a spy," he said. "You are not a Drabblovian. Stand away from your partner. Do not make any sudden movements or you will cease to exist."

Once again, I was sweating. Before I had time to react, the guard grabbed my hand and pulled. To my horror, the baby finger popped right off. No blood, nothing. I'm going to faint, I thought.

"Kerboskian spies," the guard cried out. "I bet that eye is fake too."

"This one must have stolen the top secret stink bomb antidote," yelled another guard, his words muffled by his gas mask.

"I can explain," I said again and again, but no one was listening. Jamie groaned. He was coming around. Guards were helping the president of Drabblova back into his overstuffed chair. The president of Kerbosky was back in suspended animation, his mouth frozen open, probably in the middle of mouthing his favorite word: pizza. No one had bothered to order him a Hawaiian Supreme.

Guards yanked us across the room to the president's desk. My other sixth finger had been torn off and so had Jamie's. The captain of the guards saluted in Drabblovian fashion. "Mr. President," he said, "shall we terminate the prisoners?"

The president nodded and the guards pulled us away. "No," I yelled, "I'm not a spy." Clover Elementary seemed a billion light years away.

The president motioned for the guards to stop. "I have a better plan," he said. I didn't like the sound of those words. "They are Kerboskians, enemies and spies, but they can still be of use to us. Take them to the below ground secure laboratory where our top secret experiments are carried out." The president wrote a brief note and handed it to the captain of the guards. He was smiling again. In fact, he looked quite cheerful. "Yes," he said, "this will prove very amusing. Bring me the results as soon as possible. How convenient of you to drop in," he said to us. "You are exactly what we need to make our final preparations for the termination of Kerbosky."

"But!" Jamie shouted.

"But!" I shouted. Of course, it was no use.

The president of Drabblova had turned away. He had started to giggle and then to guffaw. "Make mine with everything," he squealed. "They will be eating out my hand, every Kerboskian on that miserable little planet. Take these prisoners away at once!"

I gulped and stared at Jamie. He hadn't said a word as the guards took away his communications device. He still looked a little green. I knew we should have had a backup plan. The guards pushed us into a tiny room that turned out to be an elevator which whizzed downwards. No elegant escalator for condemned prisoners. Down and down, we sped until I felt dizzy. Dr. Freedelhum had abandoned us. He was probably deep into pizza by now. No one in the whole universe was going to save us. If only I could wish myself back to the playground at Clover Elementary.

As we descended my thoughts grew ever gloomier. What was this top secret laboratory? And what were the Drabblovians going to do to us? Kerboskians and Drabblovians had hated each other for thousands of years.

It was like Jamie had said to me, "You just get used to hating someone. It's like a bad habit." I thought about Chris and Darryl and the others. Sometimes I hated them and I sure as heck figured they hated me big time. This was a habit too, but how did you go about breaking it? Maybe the Drabblovians had been planning horrible things to do to Kerboskians for all that time. I tried to think of a plan to escape, but my brain was like mush. With a tiny bump, the elevator hit the bottom and the door slid open. My heart beat hard against my chest. I began to shake.

Jamie turned to me and uttered his first words since he had said hit the deck and set off the stink bomb. "I'm sorry, Robbie" he said. "It wasn't a very good plan, after all."

# Chapter Ten

Jamie and I sat on a hard bench in a cell. The Drabblovians didn't go in for ornate color schemes for mere prisoners. The walls and floor were dingy gray and the bench matched. It could have been any old cell, anywhere in the universe. There was nothing else in the room, not even a window. A light panel was fixed into the ceiling, but the light it gave was dim, the kind that made your father say, "Sit by a different light. You're going to ruin your eyesight."

Jamie and I looked at each other. We gulped. I wondered if he was thinking the same thing as me. Were we about to have our last few minutes on—I was thinking of on Earth, but this would be our last few minutes in the universe. My imagination was full of terrible images about what the Drabblovians were going to do with us. Would it involve a lot of blood? I wondered. It had been bad enough when my sister Mary got that major nosebleed and had to be taken to the clinic to have her nose packed.

Jamie was looking around the cell. I was hoping he'd have some neat plan in the back of his brain. After all, he'd had a private robot tutor all those years and was a computer whiz. But when he opened his mouth, I knew there was no hope. "There is no way out of here, Robbie," he said.

I sighed and wondered if crying or screaming, "I'm too young to die!" would help. "You mean it's all over?" I asked, grabbing him by the lapels of his shocking pink and slime green uniform. Jamie didn't resist. He had given up. "You said you understood the Drabblovians. You have to reason with them. Whole countries settle problems and make peace treaties. I'm only eleven years old. I'm a minor. When you do something bad on Earth and you're only eleven, the school calls your parents and you get a lecture and grounding from the TV for a week."

Jamie said nothing. I gripped more tightly. After a very long time, he replied, "Kerboskians and Drabblovians have hated each other for thousands of years. In fact, since we both got space flight and discovered each other. There is no way to reason with a Drabblovian." He fell silent again and pulled a piece of fluff off his shiny uniform.

"You can't give up now!" I shouted, letting go of his lapels. "The Drabblovians are people too. Are they cruel enough to kill innocent kids?" Jamie's look assured me that they were.

I was shaking. Jamie was supposed to have all the bright ideas. He had made up this great scheme to get the president of Kerbosky back. Now he was sitting like a lump on a gray bench, waiting for the Drabblovians to do indescribable things to us. No amount of pizza was worth this.

"Well," I said at last, "I'm not giving up. I'd at least like to finish grade six before my life is over. I would like to tease my sister one more time."

I clasped my chin in my hand and thought. I was supposed to be a pretty smart kid, at least in math, and I'd seen a lot of spy shows, but nothing came to me. I pictured the playground at Clover Elementary. Maybe Mrs. Cardwell was having math period right now. Maybe it was my turn to do the special math program on the Successmaker. Now I'd never learn more about the laws of probability. If I were back on Earth I could have tried to calculate the probability of getting into a fix like the one I was in right now. Probably, no computer could work that one out.

I was still pondering when the door of our cell slid open, revealing six guards with atomic blasters. "Kerboskian spies," said the first, "stand up and follow us. Quick march!"

I quick marched. You would too, if a guard had an atomic blaster pointed at your brain, no matter how silly his uniform looked. Jamie was silent, but I demanded, "Where are you taking us?"

One of the guards jabbed the blaster against my back. "Silence!" he ordered. His three eyes met mine. He meant business. My mouth snapped shut. Between the guards, weapons poised, we traveled down corridors until at last we came to a large door. With a sinking heart, I read the sign: *TOP SECRET LABORATORY. ALL UN-AUTHORIZED PERSONNEL KEEP OUT.*

The guard pushed a computer card into the lock and spoke briefly into an intercom. Dread almost overcame me as the large door slid open. The guards shoved us into a sparkling white room. Scientists were everywhere. They did not wear starched white lab coats like Dr. Freedelhum's. Sure, they had lab coats on and they did look pretty starched, but every one was a different color, like someone had made up a rule: no matching lab coats. Computers were everywhere too, in every color imaginable. Only the walls were white.

One of the scientists approached us. His lab coat was the pale yellow of a newborn chick. He rubbed his hands together and grinned as he read the president's note. "What luck!" he said. "Things could not have worked out better for the final experiment."

"Prepare the meal," he ordered the other scientists, who whizzed around in their multicolored lab coats, pushing computer buttons with their six fingers and blinking their three eyes.

"I have a treat for you Kerboskian spies," he said, smiling grimly at us, "a taste of Drabblovian cooking."

With a sinking feeling I remembered Jamie's advice, "Whatever you do, don't eat the food." Could it be worse than sushi or onions? I wondered.

"I'm not exactly hungry, just eaten, you know," I said to the head scientist. "Do you think I could take a rain check on that meal, although I'm sure it's delicious?" I had this insane hope that good manners might make a difference.

The scientist in the pale yellow lab coat didn't even seem to have heard. "Set the table," he ordered, "and get that third eye off the prisoners. It looks ridiculous on Kerboskian spies." With that, a guard snatched away my third eye. I felt woozy as my vision got used to being its normal self again. I glanced at Jamie, but his eyes were fixed on the floor. I tried again.

"I'm not from Kerbosky," I said. "I'm from the planet Earth, you know the place that made pizza famous across the universe."

The scientist in the yellow lab coat glanced at me and smiled, but it wasn't a friendly smile. "Nice try, Kerboskian spy. You have more imagination than I thought, but no go." He turned to the nearest guard. "Take the Kerboskian spies to our special top secret kitchen."

We were propelled into a smaller room by the guards and their blasters. "Wait!" I shouted. "Give me a lie detector test. I can prove I'm from Earth. Ask me anything. I can name all the oceans, the continents. I can name the president of the United States."

The guards looked mildly irritated. "Be quiet, Kerboskian spy," they said.

A scientist in a pink lab coat nudged a scientist in a purple lab coat. "I am going to enjoy this so much," he said.

The last meal of my life was going to be a Drabblovian special. I might get myself poisoned before they had a chance to do away with me. Was this the part where I got to yell, "Mom, Dad, help me! I'm having a terrible nightmare. AND I CAN'T WAKE UP!"?

# Chapter Eleven

You know how on a Friday when Mom and Dad have been totally fried at work and everyone's too tired to make supper and you order out for pizza? First there's the big argument about whether to have double pepperoni or Hawaiian. Then there's the thickness of crust argument, but then you finally settle and Dad phones and you wait for the pizza, practically foaming at the mouth with hunger. When the delivery person brings the pizza box in it smells so good. The whole family noshes down on pizza, but somehow one tiny piece is left. Maybe it's because no one could figure out how it would be fair if someone got the very last piece and it gets put in the fridge.

Anyhow, a long time later, like maybe a couple of weeks, you're rooting around in the fridge after school and you find this dried-up piece of pizza. Well, it's begun to smell a little off, but you're really hungry. There you are, holding the wrinkled piece of pizza in your hand, debating about whether to take a bite or not, when Mom rushes over shouting, "Robbie Packford, throw that pizza in the garbage at once. What is the matter with you? Do you want to get food poisoning?"

Keep that scene in mind. It will help you to understand the essentials of Drabblovian cooking. Sure it was pizza they were going to serve Jamie and me for our last meal in the universe. But they hadn't been able to get the computer program from the Kerboskians and Drabblova was a little far away to order out from Earth. For some reason, Earth pizzerias didn't deliver outside of a four galaxy radius. The head scientist was smiling as he put the pizza platter in front of us. The scientists in the purple and pink lab coats tied huge polka-dot napkins around our necks. They played soft computer music in the background. It might have been the pizza place down the road, except for one thing.

What lay on the table steaming in front of us was like no food I'd ever seen before. And the smell wafting up from that platter made me retch. The thing on the plate was round. It did have a sort of crust underneath and gooey bright orange stuff on top that maybe was like cheese, but the resemblance to food ended there.

I take it back. There are lots worse things to eat than onions and sushi. And guess what? They're all on Drabblova.

The head scientist in the pale yellow lab coat pressed a fork-like implement with two big tines into my hand. I didn't have to ask what it was for. The scientist's three eyes glinted. He was like some waiter from a horror movie. I had never known before that you could torture people by feeding them. Jamie had turned the same shade of green as when the stink bomb had gone off. He held his fork in the air, looking like he didn't have a clue what it was for. I thought about telling them I was Chinese and could only eat with chopsticks.

The guards moved closer. All their eyes stared at us. Their atomic blasters were poised. "Enjoy," said one. "Drabblovian cooking is famous around the whole galaxy."

"It would make a winning rat poison," said Jamie, staring at the mess in front of him. His fork wavered in the air.

If only I could think of a reason not to eat this food. "Allergies," I said firmly, "I have allergies. I think I'm lactose intolerant and I'm sure I'm deathly allergic to the green stuff under the orange stuff." I continued to stare at the plate. Was it my imagination or was the orange goo beginning to move all by itself?

The head scientist swished forward. "No more stalling, Kerboskian spies," he said. "Eat up and we'll soon know if you will be addicted to Drabblovian special deluxe pizza."

"More like poisoned than addicted," I said to myself. The revolting pizza swam before my eyes. Its stench strengthened and my gag reflex started acting up again. The nearest guard grabbed my hand and pushed the fork into the gooey orange guck.

"Try it. You'll like it," he said. "I'll even cut it into bite-sized chunks for your dining pleasure."

My arm went rigid. I couldn't force the fork into the gross mess on my plate. "Let me help you," said the guard, grabbing the fork from my hand. He speared a big piece and pressed it towards my mouth.

"This is not pizza!" I shouted. "It's garbage. No one in his right mind would eat it."

"Open that little mouth," said the guard, "and let the nice pizza slide down the red lane."

I clamped my jaws shut. What an undignified end to my short life: poisoned by Drabblovian pizza! The guard pressed the foul-smelling pizza against my lips and clenched teeth. "Open wide, Kerboskian spy," he said. "You will just love this taste sensation."

Now, you won't believe what happened next. Me neither. You know how, in those murder mystery movies when the great detective is about to tell who committed the murder? Mrs. Cardwell calls that the denouement. Anyhow, just as the detective is about to say the murderer's name and everyone is on the edge of their seats, suddenly—*Pow!*—all the lights go off. That is what happened next. The lights went out, and in the windowless top-secret kitchen it became black as black. I could hear everyone gasp including me.

Then, silence.

# Chapter Twelve

Here are some of the things that I did not see when the lights went back on.

I did not see the president of Kerbosky who had mysteriously escaped from suspended animation and come to save us. I did not see an army of Kerboskian robots, atomic blasters poised, ready to save the day. I didn't even see the man from the pizza delivery place around the corner from Clover School saying, "Okay, who's the wise guy who just ordered thirty-seven deluxe large pizzas with everything?"

What I did see made the breath freeze right inside my body because now I knew for sure that we were never going to be saved. I would spend my last moment in the universe swallowing a bite of Drabblovian pizza. No one on Earth would ever know what happened to me. One day, there was Robbie, a pretty average kid in grade six. Then, nothing.

Even the guards were staring. The one who had been trying to force-feed me dropped his forklike implement in amazement, and the orange goo and green slime slithered to the floor.

"Who is it?" the guards demanded, grabbing for their blasters.

Jamie stood up as if he had awakened from a long sleep. "It's Dr. Freedelhum," he said. "Kerbosky's leading scientist."

I gasped again. If Dr. Freedelhum was Kerbosky's leading scientist, we were in even more trouble than I had figured. Compared to Dr. Freedelhum, the Drabblovian scientists in their rainbow-hued lab coats looked almost normal. Dr. Freedelhum must have teleported down from the spaceship because there he was in front of us, big as life, smiling through the wiggly pince-nez. Dr. Freedelhum was not wearing his starched white lab coat, I'm embarrassed to say.

He was still wearing his frog and ducky pajamas. And he was clutching Teddy in one hand and Froggy in the other.

Cries sprang up from the collection of scientists and guards. "Who is that?" "What are those animals he's holding?" "Are they dangerous?" "And what the heck is he wearing?"

"It's Dr. Freedelhum in his frog and ducky pj's with his private collection of stuffed toys from Earth," I whispered, but no one paid attention.

The Drabblovian guards were all business in their shocking pink and slime green uniforms. Their atomic blasters pointed straight at Dr. Freedelhum.

"Wait," he cried, holding up Teddy and Froggy. "I have had a revelation. Now I understand it all."

The six fingers of each guard curled around his atomic blaster and felt for the trigger. Dr. Freedelhum didn't look scared. That's because he's totally nuts, I thought. Only a crazy person would smile with a dozen atomic blasters ready to blast his atoms into nothingness in point one seconds.

"Hold your fire!" The command came from the head scientist in the pale yellow lab coat. The guards froze, but their fingers did not move from the triggers of the atomic blasters. "I must consult the president," he said, "before we execute the intruder."

"Goody!" said Dr. Freedelhum. "I have to explain it all to him so he can understand too." He clutched Teddy and Froggy tighter. "And it's all because of my dear friends here," he said. At first, I thought he meant Jamie and me, but no, it was worse, much worse. He meant Teddy and Froggy. Dr. Freedelhum used to think that Teddy and Froggy were giving him secret messages. Now he thought that they revealed the solution for the planet of Drab-blova. I wondered if this was the final stage of pizzamania.

I glanced at Jamie. He was staring at Dr. Freedelhum, just as surprised as I was.

The scientists in the pink and purple lab coats were frowning. "This intruder is spoiling our experiment," they complained, "and we were just getting to the good part."

"Hold the pizza," ordered the head scientist. "It's not going anywhere and neither are these prisoners. We'll save it for their midnight snack."

My heart sank. My fate had not changed. It was only being put off a little.

"I have to see the president," Dr. Freedelhum shouted. "Teddy and Froggy can explain everything. I promise you the president will be very happy with their news."

Jamie was rolling his eyes and twitching his fingers. I think he was trying to get Dr. Freedelhum's attention. He was trying to mouth the words, "Beam us up," but Dr. Freedelhum was not paying even the slightest attention. He was smiling at Teddy and Froggy and holding them up for the guards to see.

The guards still looked puzzled, but at least they had figured out that Dr. Freedelhum's stuffed animals weren't real or some hidden weapon. It was probably only Dr. Freedelhum's craziness that prevented them from blasting him right on the spot. I could tell this wasn't exactly a situation they had been trained for. The guards' eyes moved between Dr. Freedelhum and the head scientist in the pale yellow lab coat. Dr. Freedelhum was giggling by this time and making Teddy wave his paw at the blasters. The most unsettling thing was that Dr. Freedelhum appeared totally unafraid. I remembered in the book we were reading at school, when Mrs. Cardwell had talked to us about healthy fear. Now I understood. People like Dr. Freedelhum were far too crazy to be afraid. Besides, he had Teddy and Froggy to protect him.

We stood there like statues, wondering what was going to happen next. I tried smiling at the guards, but one pushed his atomic blaster up against my chest. "No, funny stuff, Kerboskian spy," he ordered.

The vision of me with the atomic blaster pressed against my chest struck Dr. Freedelhum as hilarious. He was no longer giggling. He was guffawing. "You think that boy is a Kerboskian spy?" He roared with laughter. "Froggy, did you hear that? They think Robbie is a spy." Dr. Freedelhum shook Teddy as if he were laughing too. I was not amused. I just hoped that the guard whose finger was pressed against the destruct button on the atomic blaster was. Maybe a little amusement would keep me alive a moment or two longer.

The head scientist drew closer to Dr. Freedelhum. "All right, so-called leading scientist from the planet of Kerbosky," he said, "exactly who are your co-conspirators here?"

Dr. Freedelhum held up Teddy and Froggy. "No!" shouted the head scientist. "Not those ridiculous creatures. I mean the two spies we just captured."

Dr. Freedelhum hugged Teddy and Froggy to his chest. "They won't speak to anyone but the president of Drabblova," he replied, his laughter settling down to a giggle and a snort. "But if you mean my other friends, that's Jamie, my computer whiz boy, and his friend from the planet Earth, Robbie Packford."

The head scientist frowned. I could tell by his expression that he didn't believe a word. The fact that Kerbosky's leading scientist was wearing frog and ducky pajamas and thought stuffed animals were talking to him didn't help.

The leader of the guards stepped forward. "Enough of this foolishness," he said. "Crazy or not, all three of these prisoners are Kerboskian spies and must be eliminated."

The scientists in the purple and pink lab coats rushed towards us. "Eliminate them after," they said, "but, let's have the great pizza tasting first."

The guards stared at the scientists and the scientists stared back. It was a clash of wills. Which fate would be worse, I wondered, having your atoms blasted around space or death by pizza?

Just as I was wishing to be anywhere but there, the door to the top-secret kitchen slid open and all the guards began to salute, practically dropping their atomic blasters.

"Mr. President," cooed the head scientist, "we were just about to complete the great pizza experiment with the prisoners as ordered."

"I see," answered the president, "and another has dropped in for dinner. How convenient. But he's not exactly dressed for the occasion," finished the president, staring at Dr. Freedelhum's pajamas.

"He claims to be Dr. Freedelhum, the leading scientist on Kerbosky with a revelation for you," said the head scientist.

"For me?" asked the president, looking pleased. Dr. Freedelhum waved Teddy and Froggy at the president of Drabblova.

"Except," hesitated the head scientist, "I think that Dr. Freedelhum's secret was revealed to him by those two dead animals."

The president giggled. "A secret revelation from two dead animals delivered by a mad scientist in pajamas decorated with weird creatures. I must hear this. Convene the Drabblovian Council!"

"They're frogs and duckies," I said, "totally harmless." But the shouting of the scientists drowned me out.

"Mr. President," all the scientists were crying out at the same time, "what about our great experiment?"

The president dismissed them with a wave of his hand. "Take the Kerboskian prisoners to the Council Chambers immediately," he ordered. "This is even better than 'make mine with everything.'"

# Chapter Thirteen

So here we were in front of the president of Drabblova and the council. The room seemed much bigger than before, as if the Drabblovians had evaporated a couple of walls to fit everyone in. The president's remote control instantly revealed the room where the president of Kerbosky was trapped in suspended animation. There were more overstuffed chairs with little striped tables beside them, each stripe a different color. On the tables were sculptures of eyeballs and plates of something that might have been candy in colorful wrappers.

If you thought the scientists were wearing interesting colors, you should have seen the council. It was like a kind of peacock competition with first prize going to whoever could get the most colors into one outfit. The scientists in the multicolored lab coats hovered in the background, whimpering about their great pizza experiment, but they didn't dare contradict the president who might well order them to try their own culinary concoctions. The guards in the slimy lime and shocking pink didn't take their eyes off us for a second. I could tell they expected some funny business at any moment.

And with Dr. Freedelhum standing there clutching Teddy and Froggy, you couldn't tell what could happen next. He was the only one who was unfazed. In fact, he was smiling blissfully, first at the president of Drabblova and then at the guards with their atomic blasters. He didn't seem to notice that at least a dozen atomic blasters were pointed right at his brain, or at least at what was left of his brain after pizzamania had done its worst.

"Now," ordered the president of Drabblova, standing between the two head presidential food tasters, "tell us your great secret, oh leading scientist of Kerbosky." I was sure that I detected a hint of irony in the president's voice. He seemed like a cat playing with a mouse before he devoured it in one gulp.

Before Dr. Freedelhum could speak, one of the presidential food tasters grabbed his throat, gagged and fell to the floor, unconscious. The president glared as a litter picked up the poisoned food taster and bore him from the room. No one else paid any attention. This must have been a daily occurrence on Drabblova. No wonder Jamie had warned me about the food. Immediately, another presidential food taster took the place of the one who had been poisoned. That must be the worst job on Drabblova, I thought. It would probably be easier to starve to death.

At least Dr. Freedelhum still looked confident. He looked around the room. "Where is the president of Kerbosky?" he asked. "Teddy and Froggy need him here too." Dr. Freedelhum waved Teddy's paw and shook Froggy's limp legs. "Teddy and Froggy may be replicas of Earth toys," he explained, "but the profound knowledge they hold in their tiny beings is planet shattering." Dr. Freedelhum dangled Froggy up and down. The small creature's black shiny eyes glimmered.

The president of Drabblova sighed and pressed a button under his desk, revealing the president of Kerbosky in suspended animation. Several of the guards tittered, but a stern look from the president of Drabblova silenced them.

"Teddy wants him to come out," said Dr. Freedelhum, holding up the stuffed bear.

For a crazy instant I thought this might all be some great scheme concocted by Dr. Freedelhum so that he could beam all of us back to the spaceship. But no, Dr. Freedelhum was intent on delivering Teddy and Froggy's message.

Warily, the president of Drabblova pressed another button on the remote control to delete the force field in the suspended animation chamber. The president of Kerbosky blinked. When he saw the president of Drabblova he whipped off his hat and gave a small dignified bow. "I trust you have come to your senses, Mr. President," he said. "I demand a guard of honor to conduct me back to my own planet, and perhaps we could order out for pizza along the way."

The two presidents faced one another like two angry cats with their fur standing on end. "You are still my prisoner," the president of Drabblova said. "You are only free so we may receive an amusing message from one of your countrymen."

The president of Kerbosky gasped when he saw Dr. Freedelhum and the stuffed toys. Dr. Freedelhum waved Teddy's little paw at the president. For a moment the president was silent. Then, he cried out, "Dr. Freedelhum, is that really you?"

I didn't know what astonished the president more: Teddy's little waving paw, Dr. Freedelhum's maniacal smile or the frog and ducky pajamas.

"So, this individual is the leading scientist of the planet Kerbosky?" said the president of Drabblova as another official presidential taster keeled over and had to be removed.

The president of Kerbosky nodded. "Although I do not recognize those two limp creatures he's holding, in the area of archeological culinary expertise, there is no one greater."

"That mostly means he loves to eat," Jamie whispered to me.

I nodded, wondering if the archeological part meant eating food that had hung around in the fridge for too long.

"Did you bring any pizza?" the president asked Dr. Freedelhum.

Dr. Freedelhum shook his head. "Better than that, Mr. President," he said, holding up the two stuffed toys like a beacon, "Teddy and Froggy have explained everything to me. They have told me how to solve all the problems between Kerbosky and Drabblova."

I felt compelled to interrupt. "It's pizzamania," I cried out. "Dr. Freedelhum is nuts!"

At the mention of pizza the president of Kerbosky's eyes glinted. He mouthed the words, "Make mine with everything." In another minute he was going to salivate.

"Nonetheless," said the president of Drabblova, "I will hear what Dr. Freedelhum has to say before I take my final revenge."

Jamie turned to me again. "This had better be good," he whispered. "It's our last chance. I just hope Dr. Freedelhum has a good plan up his sleeve."

I stared at Dr. Freedelhum. I could not believe that he actually had a plan up the sleeve of those pajamas.

With a gesture from the president of Drab-blova, the office fell silent. All two eyes of mine and Jamie's and the president of Kerbosky's and all three of everyone else's were trained upon Dr. Freedelhum and his stuffed animals. He gave them each a little hug before he spoke.

"Try to get comfortable, Robbie," Jamie whispered. "Knowing Dr. Freedelhum, this will take a while."

# Chapter Fourteen

Dr. Freedelhum held Teddy up in front of his face so that Teddy could do the talking. It almost did look as if the stuffed animal was talking to us. His bright button eyes seemed to shine with excitement. So for the next bit, I'll call the speaker Teddy, so as not to confuse you.

"For thousands of years," Teddy said in a growly kind of voice, "Kerboskians and Drabblovians have hated each other even though the two planets are like sisters sharing the same two suns. Life on each planet has been very different from life on the other. After the two planets discovered each other life got even more different because each planet was angry about having to share that sunlight with the other. If Drabblovians did one thing, then Kerboskians did the opposite. When Kerbosky developed robots, Drabblova created an edict never to allow robots. When Drabblova developed flying saucers, Kerboskian spacecraft had to be a different shape. Nothing could ever be the same on Kerbosky as it was on Drabblova."

Teddy stopped and asked for a glass of water. A guard brought it and Dr. Freedelhum held it to the bear's lips. It looked as if Teddy was drinking it even though his lips were stitched on his cute little face. If everyone was in the same state I was, we were all getting as crazy as Dr. Freedelhum and beginning to take his ravings seriously. The president had settled into his overstuffed chair surrounded by new official presidential tasters. Another had keeled over and had been removed. I wondered if he had been checking out some of the candy-like things from the little striped tables in the corners of the room.

"At last," said Teddy, "Drabblova saw a way to conquer Kerbosky forever and all because of the dreaded new food, pizza. That is when we had to step in to stop the conflict."

Dr. Freedelhum was holding Froggy in his other hand. Froggy's black eyes glinted beadily and his long legs hung down. I stared. They seemed to be twitching all by themselves. It didn't even look like Dr. Freedelhum was moving them. I began to wonder if he had had lessons in puppetry and being a ventriloquist because when Froggy spoke I was certain the voice was coming out of Froggy's mouth. Not only that, it didn't sound a bit like Dr. Freedelhum.

Froggy started to hog the stage. "At first Teddy drove me crazy with all that moaning about 'make mine with everything.' Then we got into a big fight."

"You almost ripped out my cute little button eyes," Teddy said.

Froggy glared at Teddy and continued. "I thought to myself, this is ridiculous. It's just like those two planets. They have been fighting for thousands of years over nothing. Can one of you tell me what Kerbosky and Drabblova have been fighting over?"

There was an uncomfortable silence in the room. I was just starting to think, Hey, these stuffed toys aren't so bad after all; they just might have something here, when suddenly the room filled with a sound like a rushing wind. Guards scrambled for their blasters. The room had been pretty crowded, what with Dr. Freedelhum, the stuffed toys, guards, scientists, councilors, two presidents and me and Jamie. In the blink of an eye, the room was so crowded that standing room only would have been an understatement.

I stared at Jamie. "It's the Kerboskian robot security guard," he whispered hoarsely. "They've come to rescue the president. They must have honed in on the energy signature from my spaceship."

Sure enough, every space in the room that wasn't occupied by a Drabblovian now had a robot in it. The robots were silver with computer screen faces that flashed numbers and symbols. They had six eye stalks on top of each of their computers screens, which could look forwards, backwards and sideways all at the same time. Some hovered just above the floor. Some whirred along on tiny wheels. Luckily robots don't have to eat, I thought to myself. I could just imagine all these robots, their eye stalks twitching, arguing to see who was going to order out for pizza. But the part that got my attention was that each one of them had an atomic blaster pointed at the Drabblovian guards in their slime green and shocking pink uniforms. Of course, Jamie and I were standing in the middle of the guards so the atomic blasters were pointed right at us too.

"I thought robots were supposed to be nice," I whispered to Jamie.

He nodded. "But only to Kerboskians."

"Surrender and return the president of Kerbosky," droned the robots. "Or we will disperse your atoms to the universe."

Naturally, the Drabblovian guards weren't in any mood to surrender. They pointed their atomic blasters right back. Soon this crowded room was going to be a big nothing, once both sides started in with the atomic blasters.

Everyone's atoms, including mine, were going to be spread across the universe and the chances of them getting back together after that, well that was something I wouldn't like to calculate.

It was a stand off, kind of like the OK Corral—Wyatt Earp and the bad guys staring each other down, each ready to draw, trigger fingers itching until, well, you know the next part. It was dead silent in the room. Even the robots had stopped their whirring wheels. It was like everyone was waiting for someone else to do something so they could start blasting.

Then I heard a crash. All eyes turned, and there were a lot of eyes if you consider that each Drabblovian had three and each robot had six perched on the tops of their eye stalks. Dr. Freedelhum had climbed up on top of the president of Drabblova's desk. He was still in his frog and ducky pajamas and clutching Teddy and Froggy. "They haven't finished yet," he moaned. "They still have something to say."

The president of Drabblova stood up. "You have nothing left to say," he said. "Neutralize that man, stuffed toys too."

Atomic blasters turned towards Dr. Free-delhum. And Froggy socked Teddy right in his button eye. "I told you this wasn't going to work," he croaked.

Unless I did something, it was curtains for Dr. Freedelhum. Without thinking, I leaped up on the table beside him. "Listen to me," I yelled. "I'm a human boy from the planet Earth, the planet that discovered pizza."

A gasp went up from the Drabblovians and equations flashed across the computer screens of the robots. "Listen to me," I shouted again, grabbing Teddy from Dr. Freedelhum before Froggy could knock out his other button eye. "Don't you see how ridiculous you all are? You're just like Teddy and Froggy. You're fighting over nothing. Stuffed animals are smarter than you. Haven't you ever heard of cooperation? I'm only in grade six and even I know all about it. Just be nice to each other."

I could hear Mrs. Cardwell's words right inside my brain. That's what she'd say after we'd had a big blowup about soccer rules on the playground and she couldn't make head nor tail of how the problem started and neither could we. "Just be nice to each other," she would say. Here I was saying the same thing to a bunch or robots and aliens with three eyes, all of them aching to blast my atoms into space.

Dr. Freedelhum grabbed Teddy back. Froggy looked a little ashamed of himself. "That's exactly what I've been trying to say," Teddy growled. "Can't we be friends?"

Teddy looked at Froggy and Froggy looked at Teddy. The stuffed toys flung their arms around each other. "I promise never to sock you in your little button eye again," croaked Froggy.

"And I will be your friend forever," growled Teddy.

For an instant the room was silent.

The president of Drabblovia cleared his throat. "We Drabblovians have the advantage, and after thousands of years we are not about to give it up."

My heart sank. This was just like Mrs. Cardwell's class. No matter how many lectures she gave about the nice stuff, even after we'd all nodded our heads like we agreed, out on the playground kids would just find sneakier ways to get after each other. The Drabblovian guards smiled and tightened their fingers on their blasters. The Kerboskian robots' eye stalks swiveled in confusion.

"You don't have the advantage!" I screamed, stamping my feet on the desk top. The words tumbled out of my mouth.

"And how is that, alien?" snarled the president of Drabblovia.

"It's because, because..." Everyone stared. Beads of sweat popped out on my face as I gaped at the atomic blasters trained on my eleven-year-old body. "Because I'm an Earthling and Earthlings can't get addicted to pizza," I yelled, shaking my fist. "Jamie downloaded my specs into his computer and it came up with a formula: the—er—Pizza Addiction Withdrawal and Prevention program. Everyone on the planet has taken the antidote by now. The robots are only the advance guard. The whole of Kerbosky is arming for war! They want their president back."

The president of Kerbosky beamed. His droopy pink mustache turned up instead of down. I was launched into the biggest whopper of my whole career. My not-handed-in-homework excuses would never compare with the words that were babbling out of my mouth. "You know how cranky people are when they are getting over a craving?" I demanded. I thought about my Aunt Rose. She's a health nut now, but she used to smoke. I remember when she was quitting how Mom would roll her eyes and say things like, "We just won't have her over till she's through this stage."

"There's a whole planet of really cranky people down there. I'm not from Drabblova and I'm not from Kerbosky. But I can only see one solution. Negotiate."

"We prefer peace. Our mission is to serve," grated the Kerboskian robots, but they did not loosen their metallic fingers from their atomic blasters. It was still a standoff.

Then both presidents stood up at once. "That weird little alien has a point," they said, eyeing each other.

"A temporary truce?" said the president of Kerbosky.

"Yes, temporary," agreed the president of Drabblovia. They shook hands solemnly.

There was the sound of clapping. Dr. Freedelhum made Teddy's paws clap and then Froggy's flippers. The president of Kerbosky applauded the stuffed toys. The president of Drabblova's twelve fingers joined in. The applause was deafening. The Drabblovian guards put away their atomic blasters. The Kerboskian robots whirred around the room, asking the Drabblovians, "How may we serve you, revered sentient beings?" Their computer faces almost looked like they were smiling.

Jamie was bent double laughing. He clapped me on the back. "We've done it, Robbie," he shouted. "The war is over." But I could only think to myself, Yeah, because I told the biggest fib in history.

The Drabblovian guards lifted Dr. Freedelhum onto their shoulders. "Like your outfit," one said. "Could we get one like it?"

The presidents were sitting side by side in the overstuffed chair. Teddy sat on the president of Kerbosky's knee and Froggy on the president of Drabblova's knee.

"We are entering a new era of interplanetary cooperation," said the president of Drabblova. "And I would like some of those pajamas with those weird creatures on them for my presidential pj collection."

"Anything for you, dear friend," said the president of Kerbosky. By this time the robots had beamed down about a hundred automatic molecular food processors and were manufacturing party treats. Everything but pizza. It was an instant party. Even the Kerboskian council had beamed down.

Robots everywhere offered food and drink, cushions, party hats, streamers, even musical instruments and free pony rides. "There must be a hundred robot spaceships in orbit around Drabblova," Jamie whispered to me. "Those robots sure know how to throw a party. Robbie, you're a hero," he added.

I shook my head and pointed to the stuffed animals. Who would believe that two stuffed animals could stop an interplanetary war? That and a little—er—not so little lie. Teddy and Froggy were still sitting on the presidents' knees. When I looked at Froggy, I could have sworn one of his black beady eyes winked at me.

It's time to leave, I thought to myself.

# Chapter Fifteen

Jamie and I leaned back in our easy chairs. The automatic molecular processor had molded them to fit our bodies. I rolled my shoulders and sighed.

Ah, comfort. No more Drabblovian pizza that looked and smelled like it had been scraped off a garbage can. No more presidential guards in slime green and shocking pink uniforms ready to blast my atoms all over space. No more robots serving party favors whether you wanted them or not. Just me and Jamie in the tiny spacecraft. Not even Dr. Freedelhum in his frog and ducky pajamas with his best buddies, Teddy and Froggy. The three of them were planetary heroes now, and a frog and ducky pajama rage was sweeping Drabblova. The automatic molecular processors just couldn't turn out those pj's fast enough. The president of Drabblova had ordered enough to wear a different set each night of the month, and that's a Drabblovian month. Naturally, each set was a different color.

Teddy and Froggy and Dr. Freedelhum were getting medals of honor from both planets for stopping a war that had gone on for thousands of years. Diplomats were drawing up terms for a peace treaty. Dr. Freedelhum was also about to be granted an honorary doctorate from the University of Drabblova for his research in alien foods.

As he said to us over the deep space communicator, "Robbie and Jamie, my new mission in life is to revitalize the taste buds of every person on the planet of Drabblova. They haven't had a decent meal in over four thousand years. It will be hard work, but I am prepared to dedicate myself to the task at hand."

"But Dr. Freedelhum, remember, no Earth pizza," Jamie said.

The computer readouts of my human DNA and physiology had finally helped the Kerboskians find the molecular structure of a compound that could ease the misery of pizza withdrawal, so my big lie wasn't such a big lie after all. It was kind of an in-advance truth. But I'm sure the Kerboskians didn't want that pizza nightmare ever again.

Dr. Freedelhum nodded to Jamie on the deep space communicator monitor. "My desire for pizza is gone forever," he announced. "But I am still sad about one thing."

"What's that, Dr. Freedelhum?" asked Jamie.

Dr. Freedelhum pointed to the two stuffed toys on the mantelpiece. "Teddy and Froggy haven't talked to me since I recovered from pizzamania," he said.

"You don't need them anymore," Jamie said.

"I suppose you're right," Dr. Freedelhum said. "But I will treasure them forever." He held them up to the deep space video transmitter for us to see. Each stuffed toy had two medals around its neck, one from each planet. "Jamie, you must hurry back when you've dropped off Robbie. I need an assistant for my great culinary project. Give my regards to Earthlings," he added, "even though their species invented the dreaded pizza. Over and out."

"Over and out," Jamie and I said together as the screen blinked off.

"Do you think he's really okay?" I asked.

Jamie nodded. "As okay as he ever was." He laughed. "Almost all the Kerboskians have recovered from pizzamania. I don't think they'll be trying any Earth food for a while."

"That's good," I said. "And after a whiff of that Drabblovian pizza, I don't think I'll want pizza again myself."

Jamie put us in orbit round Earth's moon. By now, I was used to the breathtaking mountains and craters below us. I imagined the moon over millions of years, its record of meteor collisions complete and unchanged. I imagined myself, Robbie Packford, head geologist, on a future trip to study the lunar craters and mountains.

Jamie broke into my thoughts. "Well, Robbie, I guess this is it." He shook my hand. "I think you're the real hero," he said.

I felt myself turning red. "Even if Earth pizza is the source of all evil?" I asked.

"We've learned our lesson, Robbie," Jamie answered, "and not just about pizza. Now Kerbosky and Drabblova are going to have to get along."

I nodded, thinking about the boys in Mrs. Cardwell's grade six class, especially Chris and Darryl and Peter, who bullied me sometimes. Getting along with them was never easy. I wondered what it was going to be like for two whole planets.

"Are you ever going to come back to Earth for a visit?" I asked.

Jamie was already fiddling with the controls that would put me back in time before this whole adventure had begun. It would be like this had never happened, except as a dream, a lucid sort of dream.

He shrugged. "You never know when Kerbosky will get into trouble again."

"You can call on me," I said. If only Jamie would move to Earth, he would be the greatest partner for a science project. We would wow Mrs. Cardwell with a project like nothing she had ever seen.

"Teleporter ready in one minute, fifty-six seconds," Jamie announced.

I walked over to the teleporter and Jamie began the countdown. It was like when I'd had my tonsils out and the doctor giving me the anesthetic told me to count backwards. My counting got slower and slower until it faded out completely. The sapphire light began to envelop me. "I'll miss you, Jamie," I called out.

Jamie turned away from the controls. He was already fading from view as my own atoms shimmered and faded. "Thanks, Robbie, for being my friend." He waved as I faded out, and then there was nothing.

When I opened my eyes, I was standing under the heritage Garry oak in the school yard. I looked up into the branches, but the light dazzled my eyes and I couldn't see a thing. The picture in my mind was clear as clear, though, of Jamie sitting in the branch, saying, "I'm back."

I rubbed my eyes and pressed my face against the tree's rough bark just as the bell rang. "Robbie Packford used to be just the class math geek," a voice called. "Now, he's in love with a tree." The boys laughed. They were moving towards the school doors. It was no use saying anything to Chris. He would just tease me more. Ignoring was best. He and his buddies had a way of making everyone else feel small and terrible about themselves.

As I came to the door, I was surprised to see Darryl standing on the steps. He hadn't followed Chris in. I wondered what he was going to say. I felt like giving him a good shove as I went by.

"Robbie," he said.

"What?" I asked, surprised. Usually, the bullies used insults instead of names.

He hesitated. "Do you want to be my partner in the science project?" he said. "I was thinking of something about space. You know a lot about it."

It was true. The only really good mark I'd gotten in grade five was for last year's space project. I had really gotten into it. It was the only project I'd handed in on time.

"My dad said he would help us with the models," finished Darryl.

I considered. Darryl was pretty smart. I never could figure out why he followed Chris around like a little slave.

"You serious?" I asked. Maybe this was a big lie like the one I'd told the Drabblovians.

Darryl nodded. "Chris just fools around and expects me to do all the work," he said. "I'm tired of it. I'd like a partner who would do equal work."

"Okay," I said, "it's a deal, but you have to agree to one thing."

"What's that?" Darryl asked.

"You can't call me math geek anymore."

"Deal," said Darryl. "I never thought it was fair that you got called names."

"But you did it too," I protested.

"Well, I won't anymore," said Darryl, and started telling me about some neat ideas for the project.

We're just like Froggy and Teddy, I thought to myself. If my experiences with Jamie and Dr. Freedelhum hadn't been lucid dreaming, maybe this was.

I pinched myself. Ouch! I was definitely awake. I had the feeling that this was going to be one of my better days. The two of us walked into school. If two whole planets could get along, maybe Darryl and I could as well.

**Heather Sander** haunted the public library as a child and still reads children's books every chance she gets. She started writing stories years ago for her now grown children and has already written eight volumes of the Robbie Packford series of which *Make Mine with Everything* is number two. Heather is an elementary school counselor who lives with her husband in Victoria, British Columbia.